D0042927

My Furry Foster Family

Murray the Ferret

by Debbi Michiko Florence
illustrated by Melanie Demmer

PICTURE WINDOW BOOKS
a capstone imprint

For ferret knowledge, to former zoo colleague
and forever friend Diane Kisich Davis — DMF

My Furry Foster Family is published by Picture Window Books, an imprint of Capstone.
1710 Roe Crest Drive, North Mankato, Minnesota 56003
www.capstonepub.com

Copyright © 2021 by Capstone. All rights reserved. No part of this publication may be
reproduced in whole or in part, or stored in a retrieval system, or transmitted in any
form or by any means, electronic, mechanical, photocopying, recording, or otherwise,
without written permission of the publisher.

**Library of Congress Cataloging-in-Publication Data is available on
the Library of Congress website.**
ISBN 978-1-5158-7091-3 (library binding)
ISBN 978-1-5158-7330-3 (paperback)
ISBN 978-1-5158-7100-2 (eBook PDF)

Summary: Since the Takano family's new foster pet, Murray the ferret, arrived at their
house, all sorts of things have gone missing: pencils, toys, socks, and more. Although
eight-year-old Kaita enjoys solving the mysteries, she worries that finding a forever
home for the lovable, furry bandit will be near impossible! Playful illustrations and
lots of sleuthing fun make this chapter book a treat for animal lovers and mystery
fans alike.

Image Credits
Melanie Demmer, 71; Roy Thomas, 70

Editorial Credits
Editor: Jill Kalz; Designer: Lori Bye; Production Specialist: Tori Abraham

Printed in the United States of America.
PA117

Table of Contents

Dad
(Tim Takano)

Mom
(Cindy Takano)

Me
(Kaita Takano)

Eraser

Ollie

Joss Lawrence,
Happy Tails
Rescue

Hannah Miller,
my best friend

CHAPTER 1

Hello, Murray!

I finished the last cheese cracker on my plate. Delicious!

Ollie, my mini dachshund, licked cracker crumbs from the floor. He's a good dog. He always likes to help clean up.

I wiped my hands on a napkin and turned to my mom. "I'm ready for my books," I said.

"You're finished with your snack already?" Mom said. "That was fast, Kaita." She handed me two books. They were about ferrets.

I flipped through the first one. I had already read both books a few times. My mom works at a bookstore. Whenever we get a new foster pet, Mom brings home books for me to read. I learn a lot from them. I learn even more when the animals come to our house.

Mom, Dad, and I are a foster family for pets. That means we take care of homeless animals until they find their forever family.

"Do you think we're ready for a ferret?" Mom asked me.

"Yes!" I said. "I've read these books so many times. All the ferret facts are right here in my head."

Yip! Yip! Yip! Ollie ran to the front door. He has good hearing. Ollie always lets us know when someone comes to our house. He barks even before the person rings the doorbell.

"That must be Joss with our new foster pet!" Mom said.

Mom and I went to the door. Ollie wagged his tail. He remembered Joss. She once fostered him. That is how we adopted Ollie from Happy Tails Rescue. After we met Joss, we wanted to be a foster family too.

"Hello, Mrs. Takano, Kaita, and Ollie," Joss said. She held a big, tall cage. Mom helped Joss carry it into the guest room. We usually keep our foster pets in there.

I hurried after them. I wanted to see the ferret!

Yip! Yip! Yip! Ollie wanted to see the new foster pet too. But he knew he had to wait. Whenever we get a new pet, Ollie has to wait until the animal gets settled. Ollie is smart. He went to my room to play with his favorite tennis ball.

"Good boy, Ollie," I said. I walked into the guest room and closed the door behind me.

A cute little ferret sat in the far corner of the cage. He was mostly brown-black, with a lighter band of fur around his belly. He looked like he was wearing an eye mask.

"Kaita, meet Murray the ferret,"
Joss said. "He's still pretty young.
The veterinarian thinks he's about
one year old."

Murray walked over to me and
stood on his hind legs.

"Hello, Murray," I said. "My name
is Kaita. I'm glad you're here."

"This is your first time with a
ferret, right?" Joss asked.

"Yes," Mom said. "But we've all
been reading books about how to
take care of one. Kaita, especially, has
read a lot the past few days."

"Where did Murray come from?"
I asked. "What happened to his
owner?"

"We don't know about Murray's first owner," Joss said. "A woman named Annie brought him to us. She found him in her backyard. She lives near a park."

"How did he get there?" I asked.

"Well, we think he either escaped from his home or someone let him go," Joss said. "We tried to find his owner but had no luck."

"Why would someone let him go?" I asked. I thought of Murray, wandering outside alone. I thought about how scared he must've been. My stomach started to hurt. "Why would someone do that, just leave him in the wild? Oh, poor Murray."

Joss nodded sadly. "I know. It's horrible," she said. "Sometimes owners let their pets go. They don't understand that these animals can't live in the wild. They are pets. They are used to being cared for."

Joss put her arm around my shoulder. "He's lucky he found Annie," she continued. "Or rather, it's lucky that Annie found him! She wanted to keep him, but Murray was too much work for her. It was good that she brought him to us."

"And now we will take care of Murray until he finds his forever home!" I said. "This is going to be awesome!"

CHAPTER 2

A Pocket-Sized Pet

I couldn't wait one more minute to hold Murray. I turned to Joss. "Can we let him out of his cage now?" I asked.

Murray pawed at the side of the cage. It was like he understood what I had asked! His nose wiggled.

"Yes, Kaita," Joss said. "You can let him out anytime."

"Cool!" I said, bouncing up and down.

"Just be sure there are no electrical cords for him to chew," Joss said. "Also, you need to watch him closely when he's out."

"Why?" I asked.

Joss grinned. "Annie learned the hard way," she said. "Murray chewed his way into her couch. Then he made a nest inside."

Mom picked up the pillows from the futon. "I guess we'd better put these away," she said.

Joss laughed and nodded. She opened the cage and took Murray out. He looked like a long Slinky toy.

"He's the same shape as Ollie,"
I said. "Long and narrow."

"That's true," Joss said. She held up
Murray, his body hanging from her
hands. "But Murray is more flexible.
Being able to bend easily lets him get
into tight spaces."

I sat on the floor, and Joss showed
me how to hold Murray. I held his
body with one arm and put my other
hand on top. He snuggled against me.

"He's so sweet," I said.

Then, quick as a flash, Murray
wiggled and popped out of my arms.
Good thing I was sitting down!
He hop-skipped around the room,
sideways and forward.

"Do you spot anything extra special about Murray?" Joss asked. "Take a good look."

I watched Murray as he ran around the room. He climbed over a basket of magazines. He sniffed the wastebasket. He ran around Mom's feet. He was fast!

"Oh," Mom said. She leaned down to look closer at Murray. "Is he missing a foot?"

I scooped Murray up. Mom was right. Our little ferret was missing his back left foot.

"Is he OK?" I asked. I didn't want him to be in pain. "How did that happen?"

"The vet checked and said Murray is fine," Joss said. "We don't know how he lost his foot. It's a mystery."

Mom went with Joss to get the rest of Murray's things from Joss' truck. I sat on the floor with Murray. I wanted to watch him run around some more.

Murray had a different idea, though. He climbed into my lap. Then he pushed his nose into the front pocket of my sweatshirt.

"Hey, Murray, what are you doing?" I asked him.

Murray kept pushing his way into the pocket. Before long, he had slid all the way in and disappeared.

I peeked inside.

Murray was curled up, with his eyes closed. He'd fallen asleep!

I cradled my pocket and walked into the living room. Mom was saying goodbye to Joss.

"Look," I said in a loud whisper. I pointed at my sweatshirt pocket.

Joss smiled. "Sweet," she said quietly. "Ferrets can be very playful, but then they get sleepy and nap. I think he's going to have fun with you, Kaita. Thank you for taking care of him."

"I'll do my best," I said.

After Joss left, I did my homework at the kitchen table. Murray seemed warm and happy inside my sweatshirt, so I let him sleep.

Ollie came into the kitchen, looking for a treat. He walked over to my chair and nudged my leg with his nose. He wagged his tail fast. That's when Murray wiggled and poked his head out of my sweatshirt pocket.

Ollie looked a little surprised.

"Be gentle, Ollie," I said. Joss had told us that Murray was OK with friendly dogs. Ollie was very friendly. We weren't worried about the two animals not getting along.

Murray crawled out of my pocket and onto my lap.

Ollie backed up. He still wagged his tail but not quite as fast as before.

Then Murray slipped to the floor. He hop-skipped sideways at Ollie.

Ollie didn't know what to do. He backed up some more. His tail wagged super slowly.

I giggled.

"Ollie, it's OK," I said. "I think Murray wants to play with you."

As soon as I said that, Murray started running around the kitchen table. Ollie watched for a second. Then he started running around the table too, chasing Murray!

Around and around they went. Sometimes, Murray would hop at Ollie, and Ollie would skid to a stop. Then they'd run the other way.

All I could do was laugh. They were too funny! Murray and my little dog were becoming fast friends.

After a while, Murray got tired. He crawled up my leg and back into my sweatshirt pocket.

"Kaita, it's time for dinner," Mom said. "Put Murray back in his cage for a bit, please."

I took Murray to the guest room and put him back in his cage. He curled up in his bed right away.

"Sleep well, Murray," I said.

I had a feeling he and I were going to have a lot of fun together.

CHAPTER 3

Fostering Fun

Murray *was* a lot of fun. He loved to run around the house. He loved to climb on things. He also loved to eat hard-boiled eggs. That was one of the snacks he could have. When it was time to put him back in his cage, I simply held out an egg treat. He always came running to me.

In my room, I made an obstacle course for Murray. I got some old cardboard boxes and cut out different-sized holes in them. I lined them up.

"OK, Murray," I said. I put him down on my bedroom floor. "What do you think of this?"

Murray sniffed the first box. He walked around and sniffed the other boxes too.

He poked his head through one of the box holes. Then he climbed inside. After a few seconds, he popped out of a hole on the other side of the box. He did the same thing in the next box and the next. Murray seemed to love the boxes!

I ran to the kitchen. Dad was making coffee. "Dad! Come see Murray!" I said.

Dad followed me to my room. We sat down on the floor by the boxes.

"He loves these boxes," I said.

We waited for Murray to pop his head out of one of them. It was quiet.

"Where is he?" Dad asked.

I slid over and looked in every box. But there was no Murray. "Oh no!" I cried. "He's not here!"

"I'm sure he's around," Dad said calmly. "Let's go check the guest room."

I sprang off the floor and ran to the guest room. I was so worried. What would Joss do if I lost a foster pet?

When I got to the doorway, my worries disappeared. Murray was in his cage. He was eating his food.

"Oh, he must have gotten hungry," I said.

Dad closed the cage. "I'm glad he's safe," he said.

I was glad too. It was a good reminder that ferrets are fast. I had to keep a closer watch on Murray when he was out of his cage.

Later that night, I couldn't find my pajama top. "I left it right here on my bed," I told Mom.

"Did you toss it in the laundry basket?" Mom asked.

"Maybe," I said. But I didn't remember doing that. I got a clean pajama top from my closet and put it on. I climbed into bed with Ollie and read my book.

*

The next morning, Dad took Ollie for a walk. I got an idea.

"Mom!" I said. "We can teach Murray how to walk on a leash. That way he won't get away from me in the house. Maybe we can take him outside too."

"That's a great idea," Mom said. "We have an old harness that is much too small for Ollie. Let's try it on Murray and see if it fits."

We walked into the guest room.
Murray was climbing around inside
his cage. I was glad he was awake.
I got him out, and Mom helped me
put the harness on Murray.

It fit!

Next, Mom clipped an old leash onto the harness. We put Murray on the floor. He twisted and turned. He tried to bite the leash.

"Hey, Murray," I said in a soft voice. "It's not so bad. Let's go for a walk. Follow me."

I walked a little and gently tugged on the leash. Murray stopped trying to bite it. He looked at me.

"Come on," I said.

Murray made a sound like he was laughing and started to follow me. It was the first time I heard him make a sound. It was so cute!

He got used to the leash quickly. We walked all over the house. It was fun taking a ferret for a walk!

After a few days, Murray got used to life with my family. Every afternoon, he slept inside my sweatshirt pocket while I did my homework. I wore that sweatshirt after school every day, just for Murray. After supper, I walked him. And he and Ollie played.

At bedtime, I let Murray run around his room for a while. I gave him a bit of hard-boiled egg. Then I put him back in his cage.

"Good night, Murray," I said. "See you in the morning!"

CHAPTER 4

What's That Smell?

One day, I decided to draw a
picture of Murray. I love to draw.
I always draw pictures of our foster
pets. It's a way to remember them
after they've found their forever
homes. I went into the guest room.
I kept my special sketchbook next to
the futon.

Murray was napping. Perfect! A sleeping Murray would make a cute picture.

I sat down on the futon and opened my sketchbook. I reached for my favorite pencil. It wasn't there. I checked to see if it had fallen onto the floor. I didn't see it.

Murray woke up. He walked to the cage door and looked at me.

I laughed. "You're right, Murray," I said. "I can draw later. Time for snuggles!"

I scooped him up and lifted him to my face. Our noses touched.

"Ew!" I said, turning my head. "You kind of stink!"

Murray blinked at me. I think I hurt his feelings.

"Sorry," I said. "You do kind of smell bad though."

I hugged Murray to me, but not close to my face. I grabbed his harness. Where was his leash? It wasn't next to his harness, where I had left it. "I sure seem to be losing a lot of things lately!" I said.

I carried Murray to the living room. Dad was doing a puzzle. Mom was at work. Sometimes she takes Ollie with her. That's where he was that day.

"Dad?" I said. "I think something is wrong with Murray. He smells funny."

Dad chuckled. "Remember what we read about ferrets and their smell?" he said.

"Oh, right," I said, nodding slowly. "Ferrets belong to the weasel family. And weasels have a strong smell. They use it to mark their territory." I wrinkled my nose.

"We also read that ferrets should have a bath once a month," Dad said. "Should we give Murray a bath today?"

"Great idea, Dad!" I said. I wanted to make sure Murray was always at his best. Someone might want to adopt him at any moment.

Dad and I got to work. We were both excited for our first ferret bath!

I got a shallow plastic box and put it in the bathtub. Dad filled the box with lukewarm water. I grabbed a small toy boat and put it in the water. Then we put Murray into the bathtub. We weren't sure how he would feel about a bath. Some ferrets don't like water.

Murray sniffed every part of the bathtub. When he got to the plastic box, he slapped the toy boat with his paw. The boat bobbed. Murray rounded his back and slapped the boat again.

"OK, buddy," I said, giggling. "Bath time."

I picked Murray up and gently placed him in the water.

Right away, Murray started paddling around. He rolled over and splashed. Someone was having a great time!

Dad handed me the special shampoo that Joss had brought. He held Murray, while I rubbed shampoo all over our foster pet's fur. I was careful not to get it in Murray's eyes or ears.

Once Murray was all soapy, Dad put him back in the water. Murray splashed around. I rinsed him off.

Bathing a ferret wasn't as hard as bathing a dog, at least. We once had a foster dog who did not want to take a bath! That was a big job!

I got a fluffy towel and wrapped Murray in it. He wiggled around inside.

"I think he wants to be on the ground," Dad said. "Put the towel down too."

I did. Murray rolled around on the towel. He looked funny with his damp fur sticking up. He burrowed under the towel. After a couple seconds, he poked his head out once, then twice. The third time, he grabbed a corner of the towel and ran out of the bathroom.

"Hey," I said, laughing. "Come back here, you thief!"

CHAPTER 5

Mystery Solved

Murray ran into the guest room. He dashed under the futon with the bath towel.

"Silly Murray," I said. "I need that towel back."

I got down on the floor and crawled to the futon. I peeked at Murray. There he was with the towel—and a bunch of other things!

"What do you have under there, Murray?" I asked.

I reached in and started pulling things out, one by one.

My pajama top.

My favorite drawing pencil.

Murray's leash.

Ollie's squeaky hot dog.

One of Mom's socks.

These were all the things that I had lost—and more!

Murray slid out and crawled into my lap. I laughed.

"I have solved the mystery of the missing things," I said. "You are the thief! I should've known it was you, you sneaky boy."

I snuggled my cleaned-up foster ferret, then put him back in his cage. I went to tell Dad my news.

"That's right," Dad said. "We read that too. Ferrets like to take things and hide them. Mom was looking all over for her sock last night."

"What about my sock?" Mom asked, walking into the room. She was back from work with Ollie.

Dad and I told her about Murray's stash under the futon.

"I'm glad you solved that mystery," Mom said. "And that reminds me, the Mystery Book Club meets at the bookstore tonight. Should we take Murray to meet them? They always love to hear a good mystery."

I nodded. "That's a good idea, Mom," I said. "We've had Murray for a few weeks now. Not a lot of people are looking for a pet ferret."

"Well, I'll let you tell the story to the club tonight, OK?" Mom said.

"OK!" I said.

*

That evening at the bookstore, I put Murray and his carrier behind the counter. I wanted to keep him a secret for a bit.

Ten people from the book club arrived. All of them loved books. They especially loved reading and talking about mysteries. I hoped at least one of them would want a pet ferret.

"Hello, mystery lovers," Mom said. "Before we start, I would like to introduce my daughter, Kaita. She has a mystery to share with you. Can you solve it?"

I stood in front of everyone and started telling my story. "One night, I noticed my pajama top was missing," I said. "I didn't move it. But I couldn't find it anywhere. The next day, I couldn't find my pencil either. Then a leash went missing. Then my dog's squeaky toy and my mom's sock disappeared. No one in my family knew what was happening."

A woman wearing a purple hat raised her hand. "Was it your dad?" she asked.

I giggled. "No," I said.

"That was a good guess, Maria," a man said. "Everyone was missing something, except for the dad."

"Can you give us a clue?" a teenage girl asked.

"I will give you a big clue," I said. I went behind the counter and brought out the carrier. I held it up so everyone could see Murray.

"We are a foster family," I continued. "We take care of pets until they find their forever homes. Murray is a ferret. We hope he finds a home, but we are also having a lot of fun with him."

Maria, the woman with the purple hat, cried, "Murray is the thief!"

The man turned in his chair. "How do you know, Maria?" he asked. "Maybe Kaita is trying to trick us."

Maria smiled wider. "I know because I used to have a ferret," she said. "Ferrets love, love, love to steal things."

"Maria, you had a ferret?" Mom asked. "I didn't know that!"

Maria nodded. "It was a long time ago," she said. "He was the best pet I ever had."

"Would you like to meet Murray?" I asked.

"I would love that," Maria said.

I opened Murray's carrier, reached in, and carefully lifted him out. Then I put him in Maria's lap.

Guess what? He curled right up and fell asleep on her!

For the rest of the meeting, Murray napped on Maria. She kept petting him and smiling at him. My heart filled with hope.

*

The next day, Maria came to our house. This time she wore an orange hat with a feather in it.

"I couldn't stop thinking about Murray," Maria said. "He was so sweet last night, sleeping in my lap."

"Joss already said you could take him home, if you'd like," Mom said. "She thinks you two would be an excellent match."

"Oh, I would like that very much," Maria said.

I handed Murray to Maria. He climbed up to her shoulder and tucked himself under her hair. He seemed very happy. And that made *me* very happy.

Saying goodbye to Murray was tough. But I was glad he had a new home. And I was extra glad he had a new home with someone who understood ferrets.

Maybe someday my family will get another ferret to foster. I never know what kind of pet will come to stay with us next!

Think About It!

1. In what ways does Murray look like and act like a thief?
2. Why does Kaita's mom think taking Murray to the Mystery Book Club meeting is a good idea?
3. Would you want a pet ferret? Why or why not?

Draw It! Write It!

1. Murray is a bit of a thief. Draw a picture of Murray with something he might steal from your house.
2. Write a short letter to Maria. Tell her all the things you think she should know about Murray.

Glossary

adopt—to take and raise as one's own

carrier—a box or bag that carries or holds something

dachshund—a type of dog with a long body and short legs

flexible—able to bend easily

foster—to give care and a safe home for a short time

futon—a thin, cotton-filled mattress used on the floor or in a wooden frame for sleeping

harness—a set of straps wrapped around a pet's body and attached to a leash

obstacle course—a set of things that someone must jump over, climb, or crawl through

territory—an area of land that an animal claims as its own to live in

veterinarian—a doctor trained to take care of animals; also called a vet

A Closer Look at Ferrets

Ferrets are members of the weasel family. They have long, narrow bodies. They are quick and flexible. They can also be a little smelly. Weasels in the wild mark their territory with strong scent glands. The smells tell other weasels to keep out of the area.

Eraser

Ferrets can make good pets, but they need special care. They love to chew and burrow and can get into hard-to-reach places. It's important that pet ferrets have time to run around. It is also important to keep an eye on them. They can get into trouble. They might chew or steal things or get stuck in couches or other narrow spaces.

Pet ferrets are curious and friendly. They can sleep on their owner's lap for long periods of time. They can be litter box-trained and learn to walk on a leash. They can also learn tricks. Before you get a ferret, be sure your state allows them as pets.

Kaita's Favorites

Kaita Takano is a made-up character. She is based on a real-life Kaita, who also fosters pets with her family.

Author Debbi Michiko Florence asked Real-Life Kaita what some of her favorite things are. Then Debbi imagined how Murray the ferret would answer the same questions.

What would *your* answers be?

What is your favorite food?

Kaita — sushi (and anything else with white rice)

Murray — boiled eggs

What is your favorite book?

Kaita – anything with monsters or scary clowns

Murray – any book I can get my teeth into (and chew)

What is your favorite game?

Kaita – *Minecraft*

Murray – taking things that belong to the Takano family and hiding them under the futon

What is your favorite thing to do outdoors?

Kaita – gardening

Murray – digging in the garden

What is your favorite thing to do indoors?

Kaita – knitting, crocheting, or watching YouTube videos

Murray – sleeping in Kaita's hoodie pocket

About the Author

Debbi Michiko Florence writes books for children in her writing studio, The Word Nest. She is an animal lover with a degree in zoology and has worked at a pet store, the Humane Society, a raptor rehabilitation center, and a zoo. She is the author of two chapter book series: Jasmine Toguchi (FSG) and Dorothy & Toto (Picture Window Books). A third-generation Japanese American and a native Californian, Debbi now lives in Connecticut with her husband, a rescue dog, a bunny, and two ducks.

About the Illustrator

Melanie Demmer is an illustrator and designer based out of Los Angeles, California. Originally from Michigan, she graduated with a BFA in illustration from the College for Creative Studies and has been creating artwork for various apparel, animation, and publishing projects ever since. When she isn't making art, Melanie enjoys writing, spending time in the great outdoors, iced tea, scary movies, and taking naps with her cat, Pepper.

Go on all the fun, furry foster adventures!

Only from Capstone!